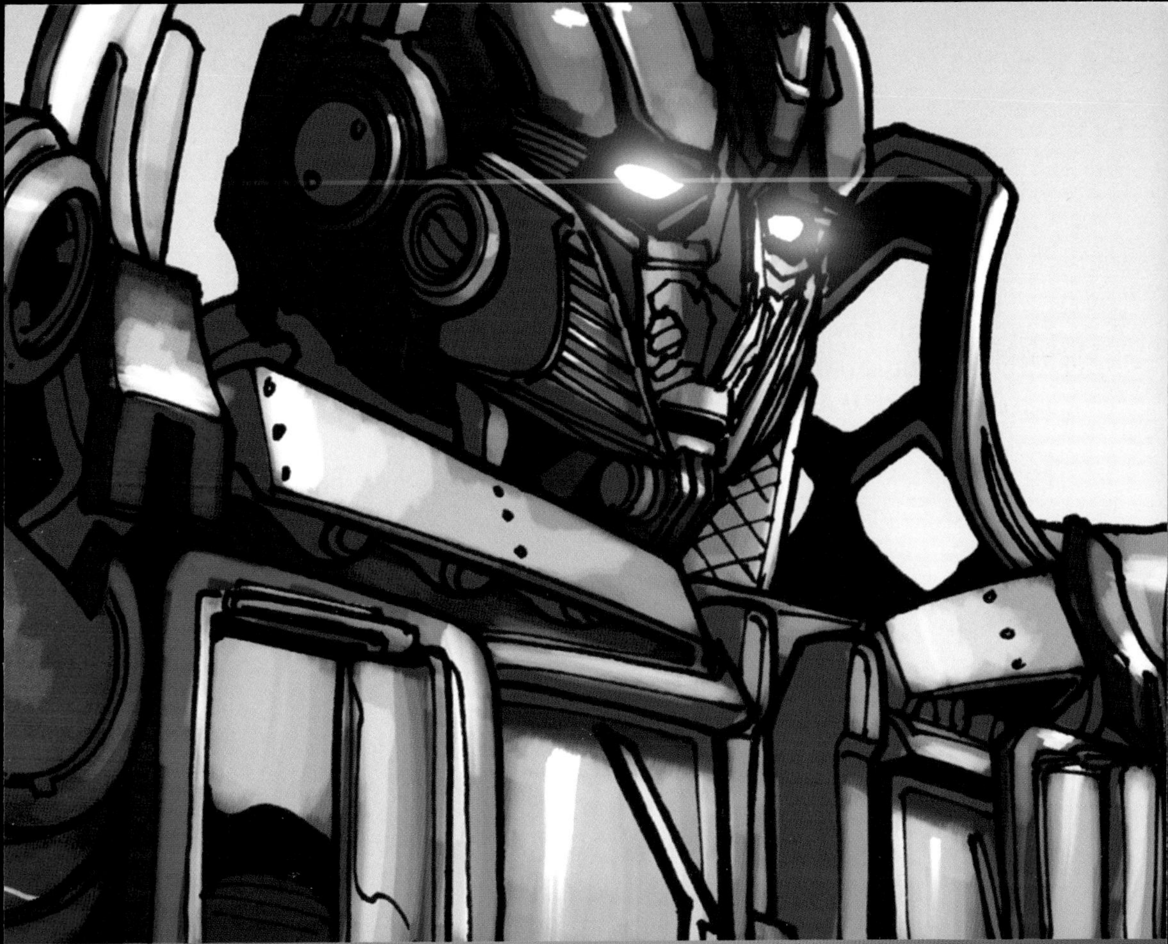

TRANSFORMERS: ALLIANCE
ISSUE NUMBER FOUR (OF FOUR)

WRITTEN BY: **CHRIS MOWRY**
ART BY: **ALEX MILNE**
COLORS BY: **JOSH PEREZ & KRIS CARTER**
LETTERS BY: **CHRIS MOWRY**
EDITS BY: **DENTON J. TIPTON & ANDY SCHMIDT**

While the AUTOBOTS and humans begin to work together as a special operations unit, numerous DECEPTICONS have begun to land on Earth. Their purpose is unclear, but they must be stopped. Is SOUNDWAVE taking control over the DECEPTICON army, or simply following orders from long ago? With the DECEPTICON scouts hiding among Earth's vehicles, can the new alliance of humans and AUTOBOTS stop them before it's too late, or will the events of CYBERTRON'S past finally come into being?

Special thanks to Hasbro's Aaron Archer, Michael Kelly, Amie Lozanski, Val Roca, Ed Lane, Michael Provost, Erin Hillman, Samantha Lomow, and Michael Verrecchia for their invaluable assistance.

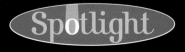

VISIT US AT
www.abdopublishing.com

Reinforced library bound edition published in 2010 by Spotlight, a division of the ABDO Group, 8000 West 78th Street, Edina, Minnesota 55439. Published by agreement with IDW Publishing. www.idwpublishing.com

Printed in the United States of America, Melrose Park, Illinois.
102009
012010

 PRINTED ON RECYCLED PAPER

Library of Congress Cataloging-in-Publication Data

Mowry, Chris.
  Alliance / written by Chris Mowry ; art by Alex Milne ; colors by Josh Perez & Kris Carter ; letters by Chris Mowry & Neil Uyetake.
    v. cm.
  "Transformers, revenge of the fallen, official movie prequel."
  ISBN 978-1-59961-717-6 (vol. 1) -- ISBN 978-1-59961-718-3 (vol. 2)
  ISBN 978-1-59961-719-0 (vol. 3) -- ISBN 978-1-59961-720-6 (vol. 4)
  1. Graphic novels. I. Milne, Alex. II. Transformers, revenge of the fallen (Motion picture) III. Title
  PZ7.7.M69Al 2010
  741.5'973--dc22
                              2009036393

All Spotlight books have reinforced library bindings and are manufactured in the United States of America.

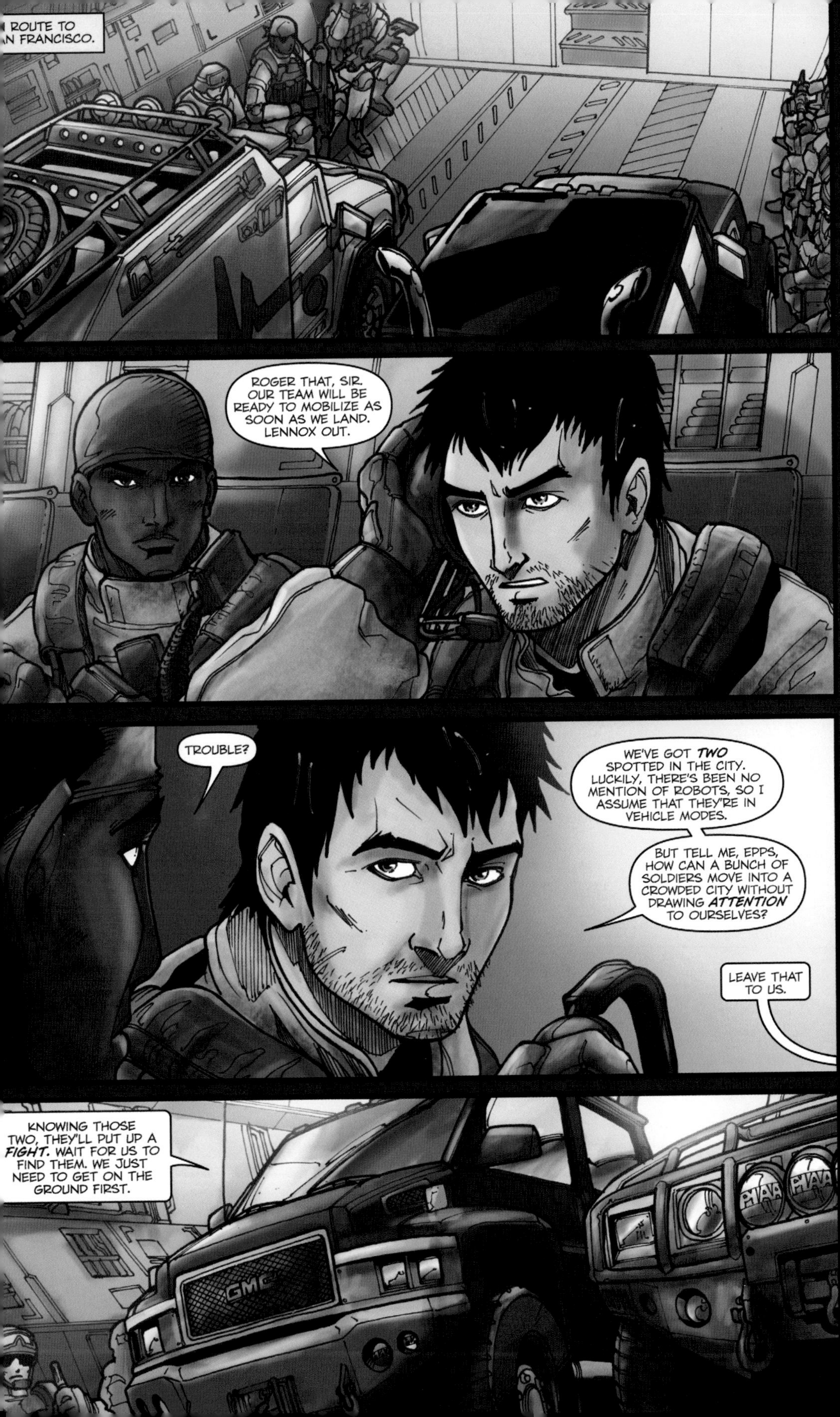

EN ROUTE TO SAN FRANCISCO.
ROGER THAT, SIR. OUR TEAM WILL BE READY TO MOBILIZE AS SOON AS WE LAND. LENNOX OUT.
TROUBLE?
WE'VE GOT TWO SPOTTED IN THE CITY. LUCKILY, THERE'S BEEN NO MENTION OF ROBOTS, SO I ASSUME THAT THEY'RE IN VEHICLE MODES.
BUT TELL ME, EPPS, HOW CAN A BUNCH OF SOLDIERS MOVE INTO A CROWDED CITY WITHOUT DRAWING ATTENTION TO OURSELVES?
LEAVE THAT TO US.
KNOWING THOSE TWO, THEY'LL PUT UP A FIGHT. WAIT FOR US TO FIND THEM. WE JUST NEED TO GET ON THE GROUND FIRST.

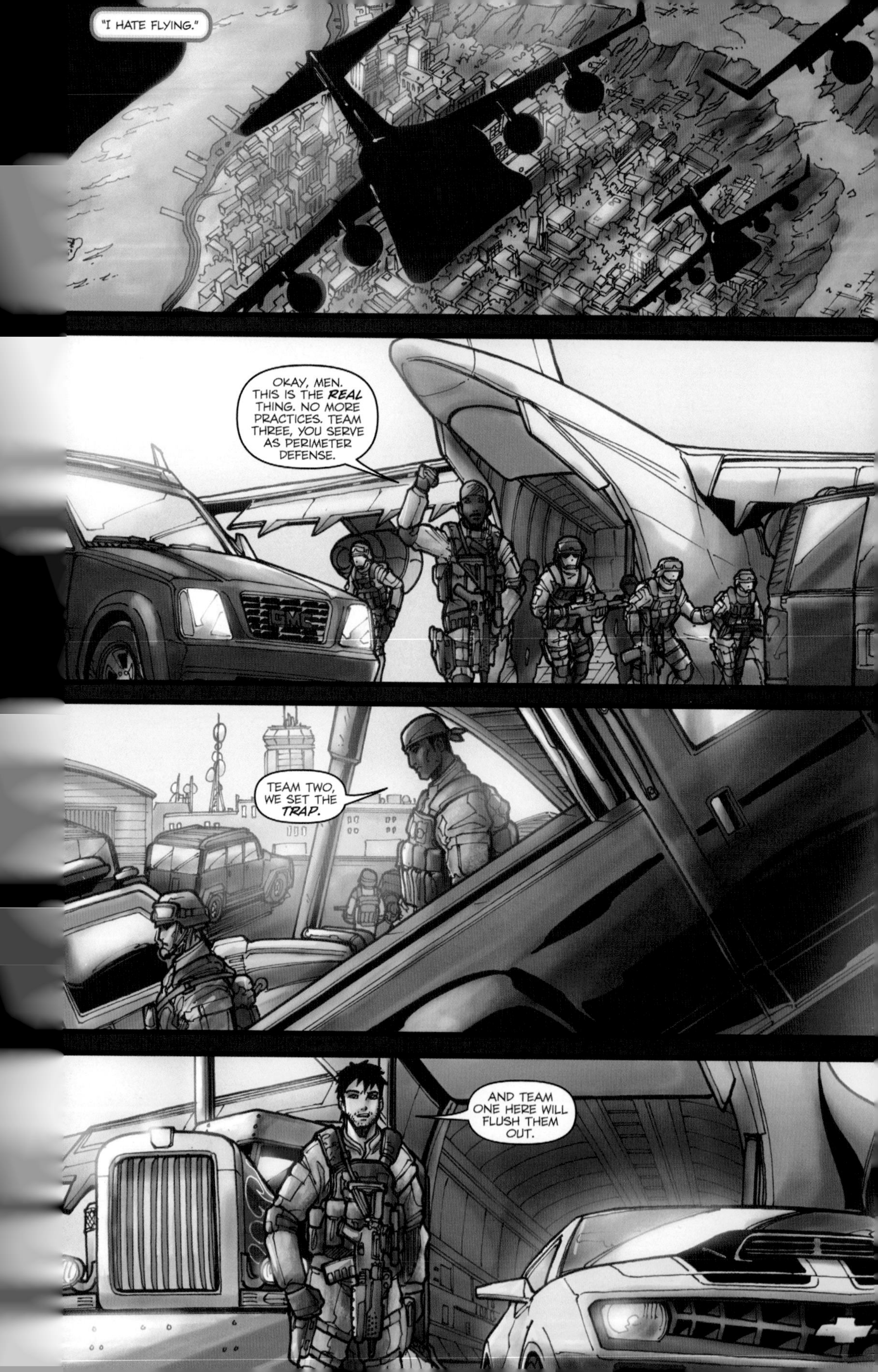
"I HATE FLYING."
OKAY, MEN. THIS IS THE REAL THING. NO MORE PRACTICES. TEAM THREE, YOU SERVE AS PERIMETER DEFENSE.
TEAM TWO, WE SET THE TRAP.
AND TEAM ONE HERE WILL FLUSH THEM OUT.

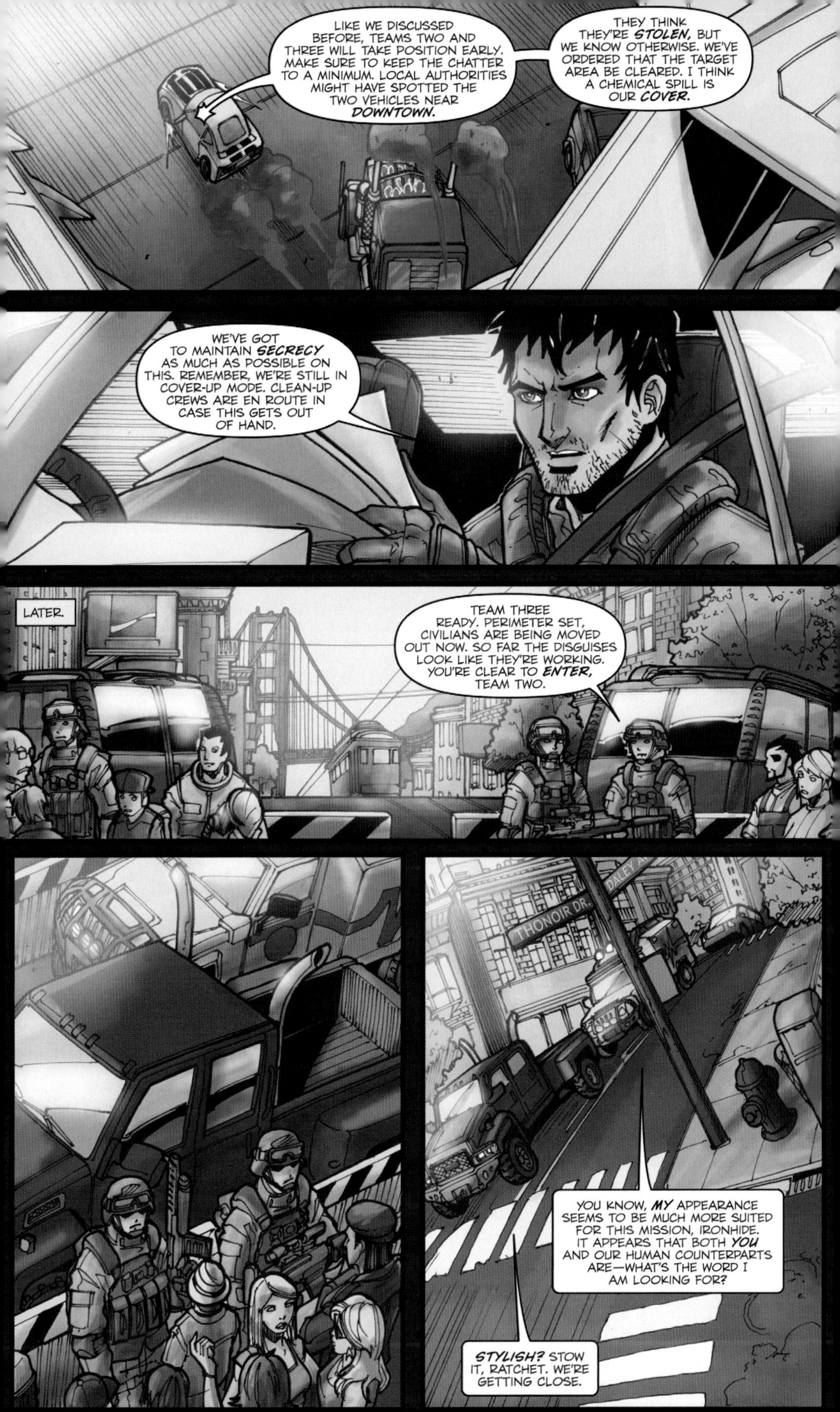
LIKE WE DISCUSSED BEFORE, TEAMS TWO AND THREE WILL TAKE POSITION EARLY. MAKE SURE TO KEEP THE CHATTER TO A MINIMUM. LOCAL AUTHORITIES MIGHT HAVE SPOTTED THE TWO VEHICLES NEAR DOWNTOWN.
THEY THINK THEY'RE STOLEN, BUT WE KNOW OTHERWISE. WE'VE ORDERED THAT THE TARGET AREA BE CLEARED. I THINK A CHEMICAL SPILL IS OUR COVER.
WE'VE GOT TO MAINTAIN SECRECY AS MUCH AS POSSIBLE ON THIS. REMEMBER, WE'RE STILL IN COVER-UP MODE. CLEAN-UP CREWS ARE EN ROUTE IN CASE THIS GETS OUT OF HAND.
LATER.
TEAM THREE READY. PERIMETER SET, CIVILIANS ARE BEING MOVED OUT NOW. SO FAR THE DISGUISES LOOK LIKE THEY'RE WORKING. YOU'RE CLEAR TO ENTER, TEAM TWO.
THONOIR DR.
DALEY
YOU KNOW, MY APPEARANCE SEEMS TO BE MUCH MORE SUITED FOR THIS MISSION, IRONHIDE. IT APPEARS THAT BOTH YOU AND OUR HUMAN COUNTERPARTS ARE—WHAT'S THE WORD I AM LOOKING FOR?
STYLISH? STOW IT, RATCHET. WE'RE GETTING CLOSE.

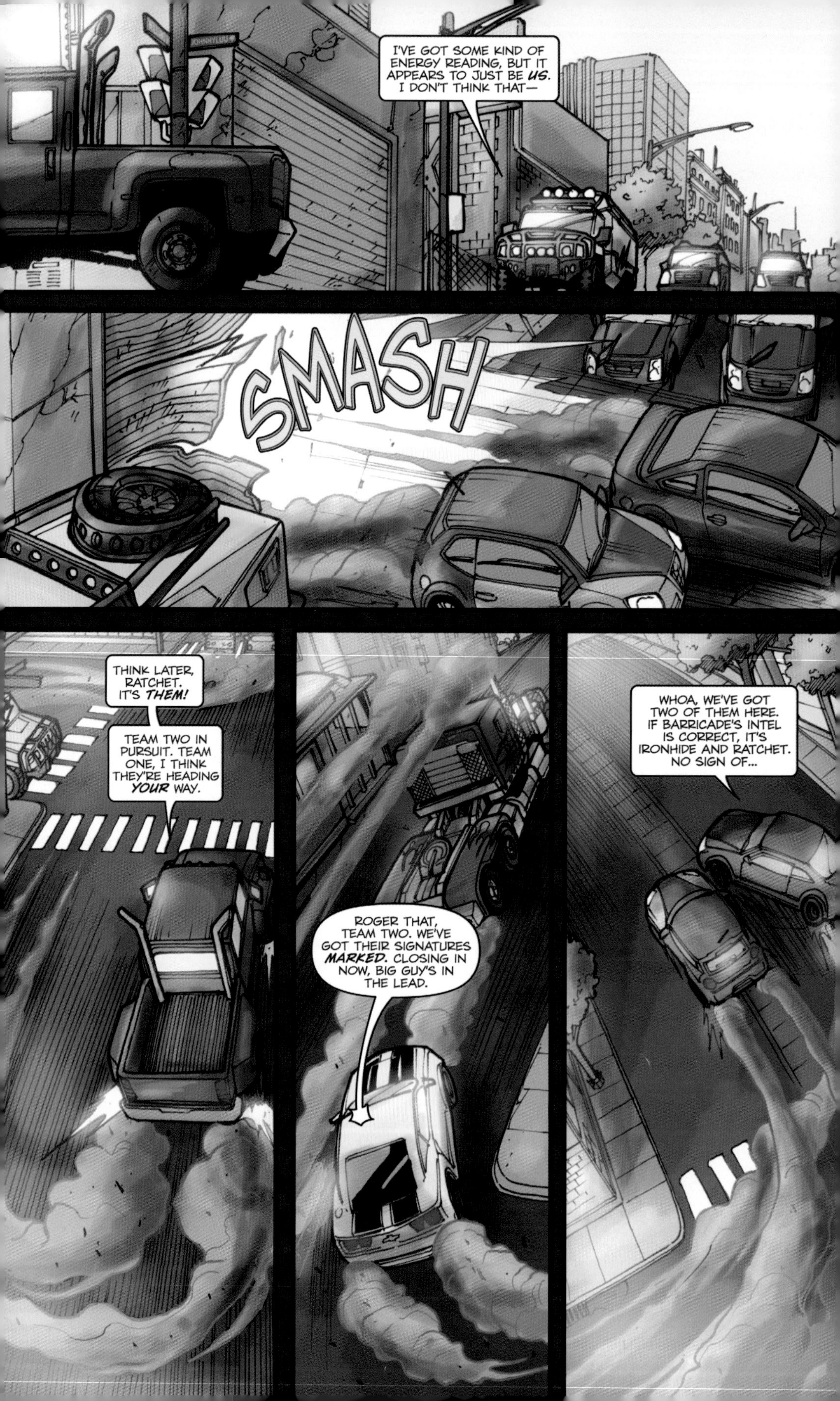
I'VE GOT SOME KIND OF ENERGY READING, BUT IT APPEARS TO JUST BE US. I DON'T THINK THAT—
SMASH
THINK LATER, RATCHET. IT'S THEM!
TEAM TWO IN PURSUIT. TEAM ONE, I THINK THEY'RE HEADING YOUR WAY.
ROGER THAT, TEAM TWO. WE'VE GOT THEIR SIGNATURES MARKED. CLOSING IN NOW, BIG GUY'S IN THE LEAD.
WHOA, WE'VE GOT TWO OF THEM HERE. IF BARRICADE'S INTEL IS CORRECT, IT'S IRONHIDE AND RATCHET. NO SIGN OF...

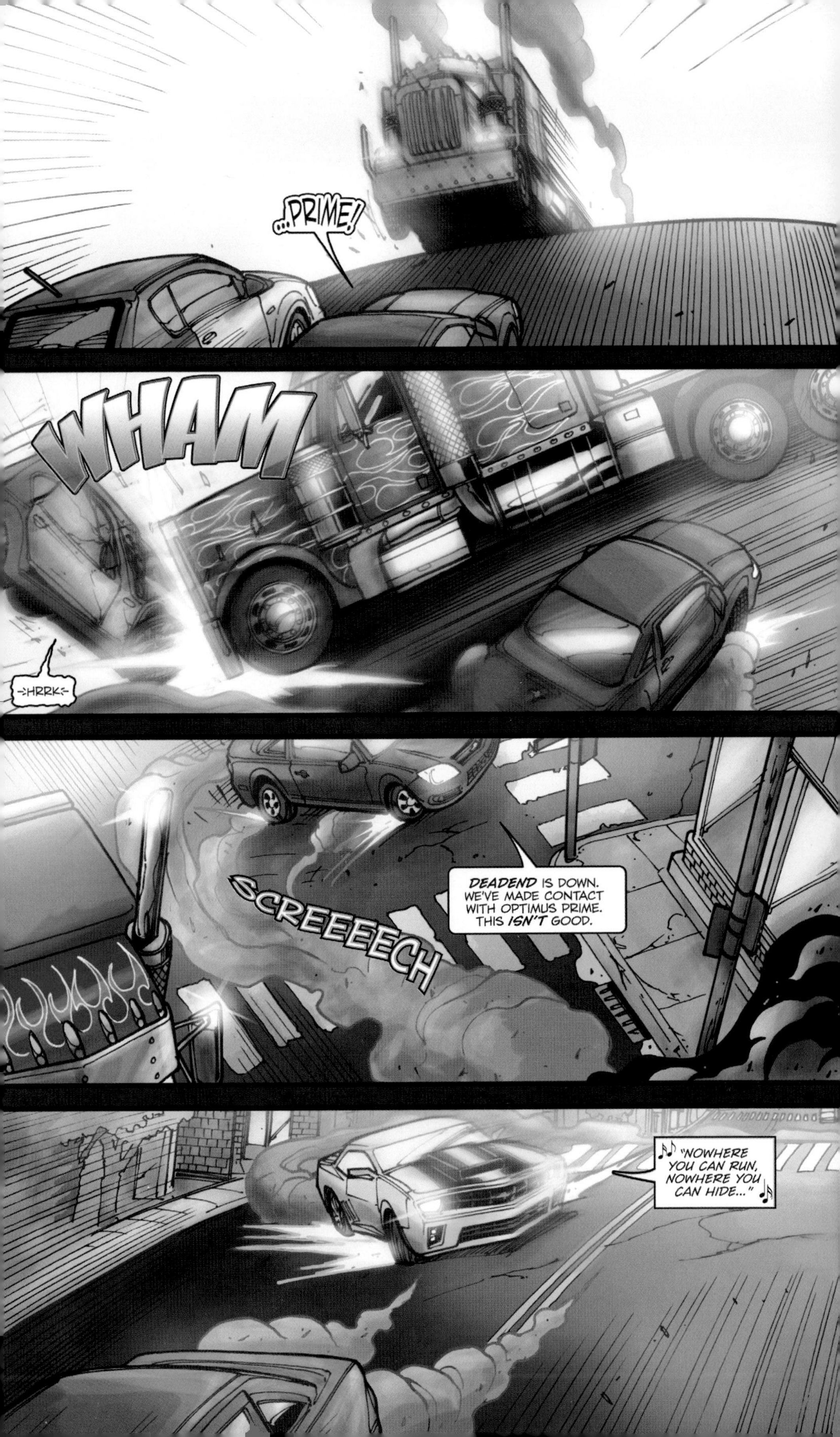
...PRIME!
WHAM
-HRRK-
SCREEEEECH
DEADEND IS DOWN. WE'VE MADE CONTACT WITH OPTIMUS PRIME. THIS ISN'T GOOD.
"NOWHERE YOU CAN RUN, NOWHERE YOU CAN HIDE..."

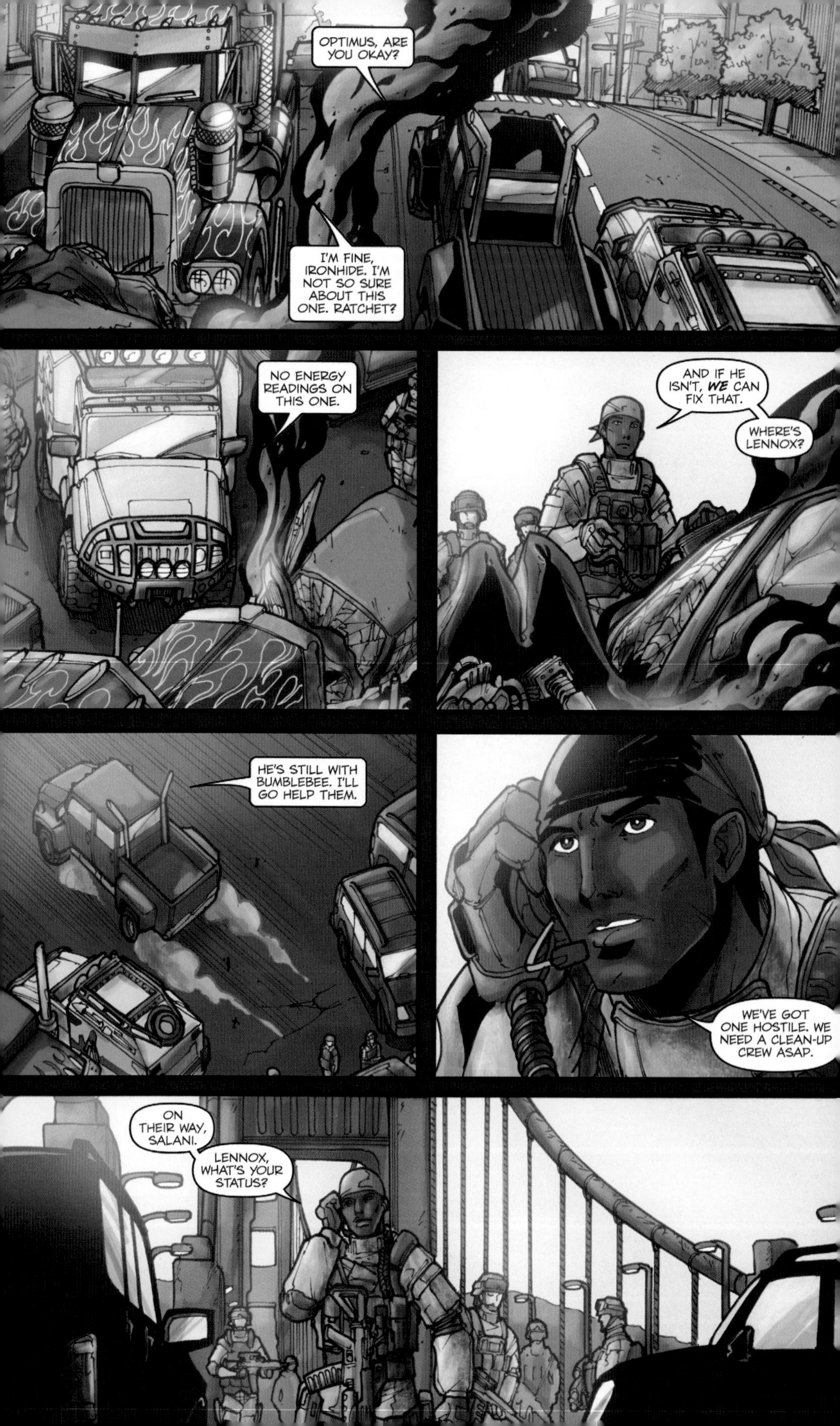
OPTIMUS, ARE YOU OKAY?
I'M FINE, IRONHIDE. I'M NOT SO SURE ABOUT THIS ONE. RATCHET?
NO ENERGY READINGS ON THIS ONE.
AND IF HE ISN'T, WE CAN FIX THAT.
WHERE'S LENNOX?
HE'S STILL WITH BUMBLEBEE. I'LL GO HELP THEM.
WE'VE GOT ONE HOSTILE. WE NEED A CLEAN-UP CREW ASAP.
ON THEIR WAY, SALANI.
LENNOX, WHAT'S YOUR STATUS?

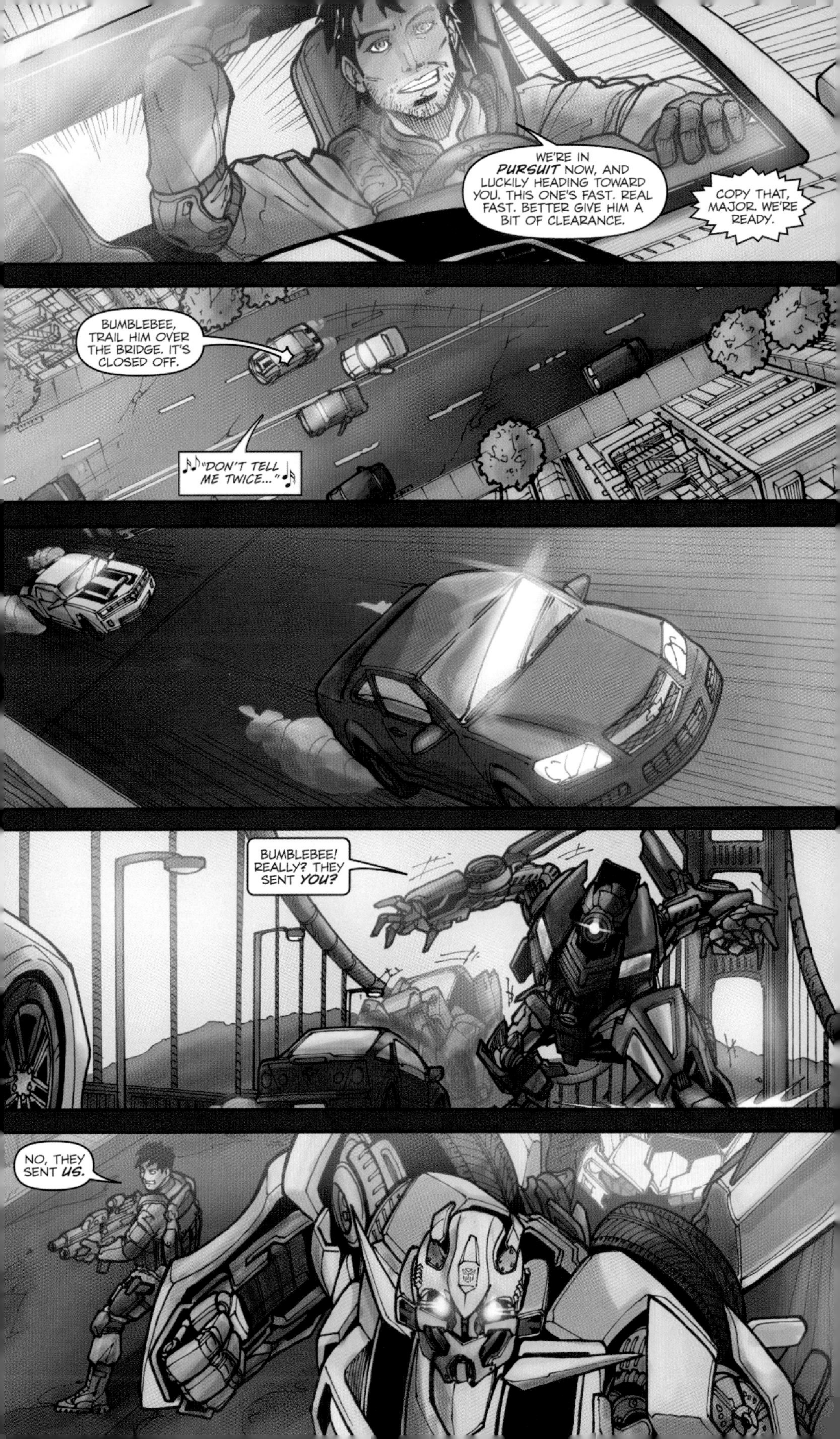
WE'RE IN *PURSUIT* NOW, AND LUCKILY HEADING TOWARD YOU. THIS ONE'S FAST. REAL FAST. BETTER GIVE HIM A BIT OF CLEARANCE.
COPY THAT, MAJOR. WE'RE READY.
BUMBLEBEE, TRAIL HIM OVER THE BRIDGE. IT'S CLOSED OFF.
♪"DON'T TELL ME TWICE..."♪
BUMBLEBEE! REALLY? THEY SENT *YOU?*
NO, THEY SENT *US.*

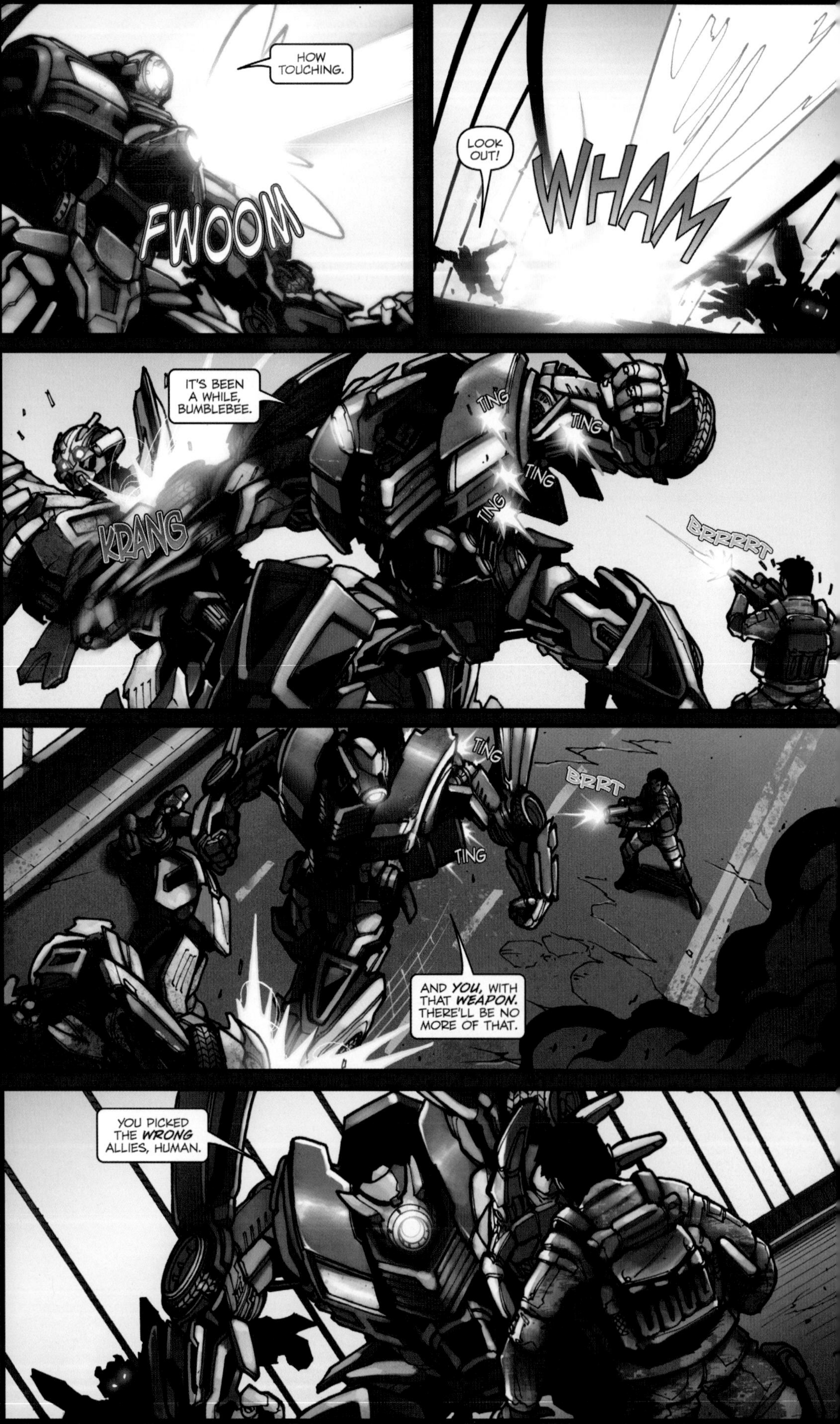
HOW TOUCHING.
FWOOM
LOOK OUT!
WHAM
IT'S BEEN A WHILE, BUMBLEBEE.
TING
TING
TING
TING
KRANG
BRRRRT
TING
BRRT
TING
AND YOU, WITH THAT WEAPON. THERE'LL BE NO MORE OF THAT.
YOU PICKED THE WRONG ALLIES, HUMAN.

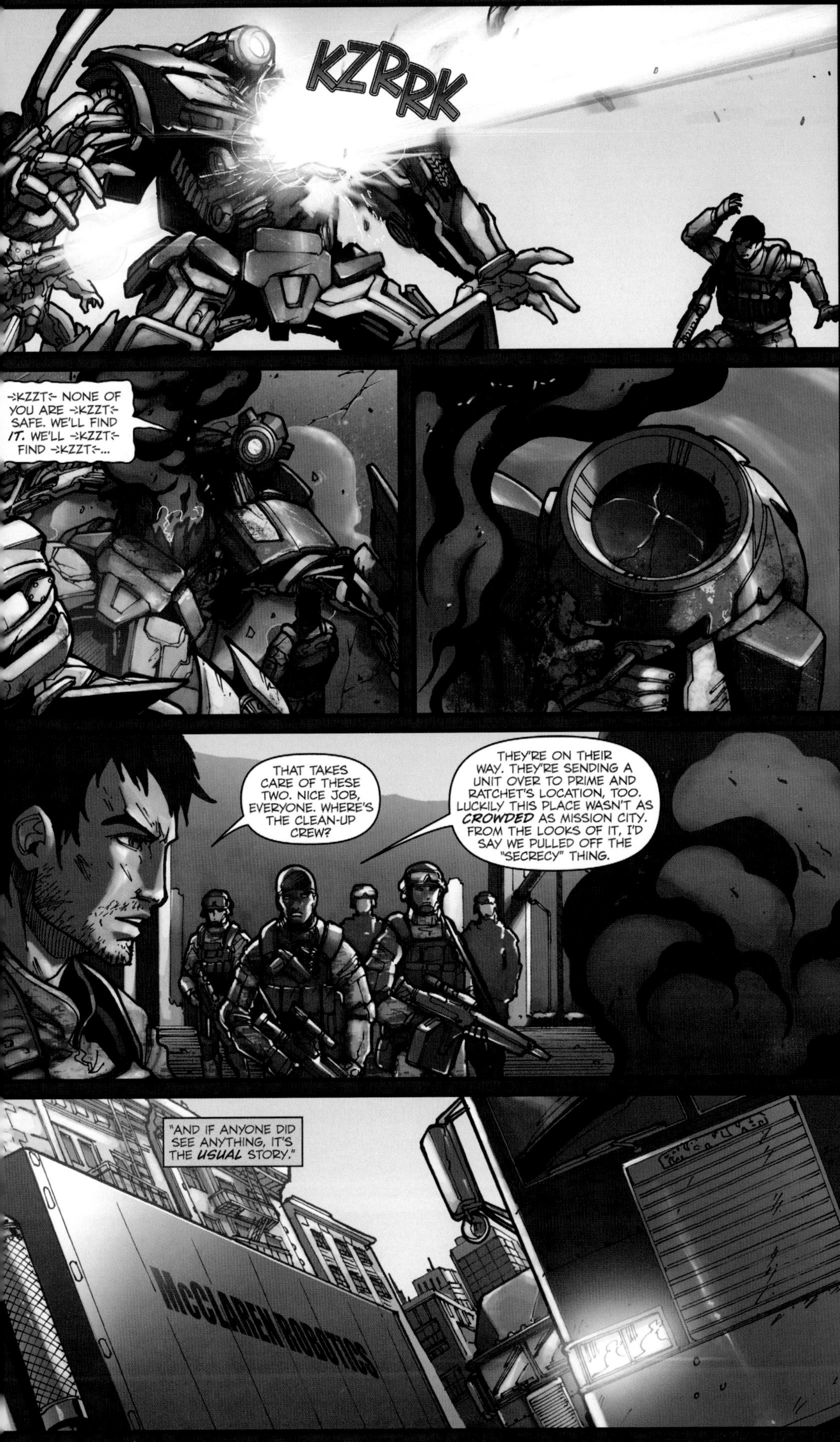
KZRRK
-KZZT- NONE OF YOU ARE -KZZT- SAFE. WE'LL FIND *IT.* WE'LL -KZZT- FIND -KZZT-...
THAT TAKES CARE OF THESE TWO. NICE JOB, EVERYONE. WHERE'S THE CLEAN-UP CREW?
THEY'RE ON THEIR WAY. THEY'RE SENDING A UNIT OVER TO PRIME AND RATCHET'S LOCATION, TOO. LUCKILY THIS PLACE WASN'T AS *CROWDED* AS MISSION CITY. FROM THE LOOKS OF IT, I'D SAY WE PULLED OFF THE "SECRECY" THING.
"AND IF ANYONE DID SEE ANYTHING, IT'S THE *USUAL* STORY."
McCLAREN ROBOTICS

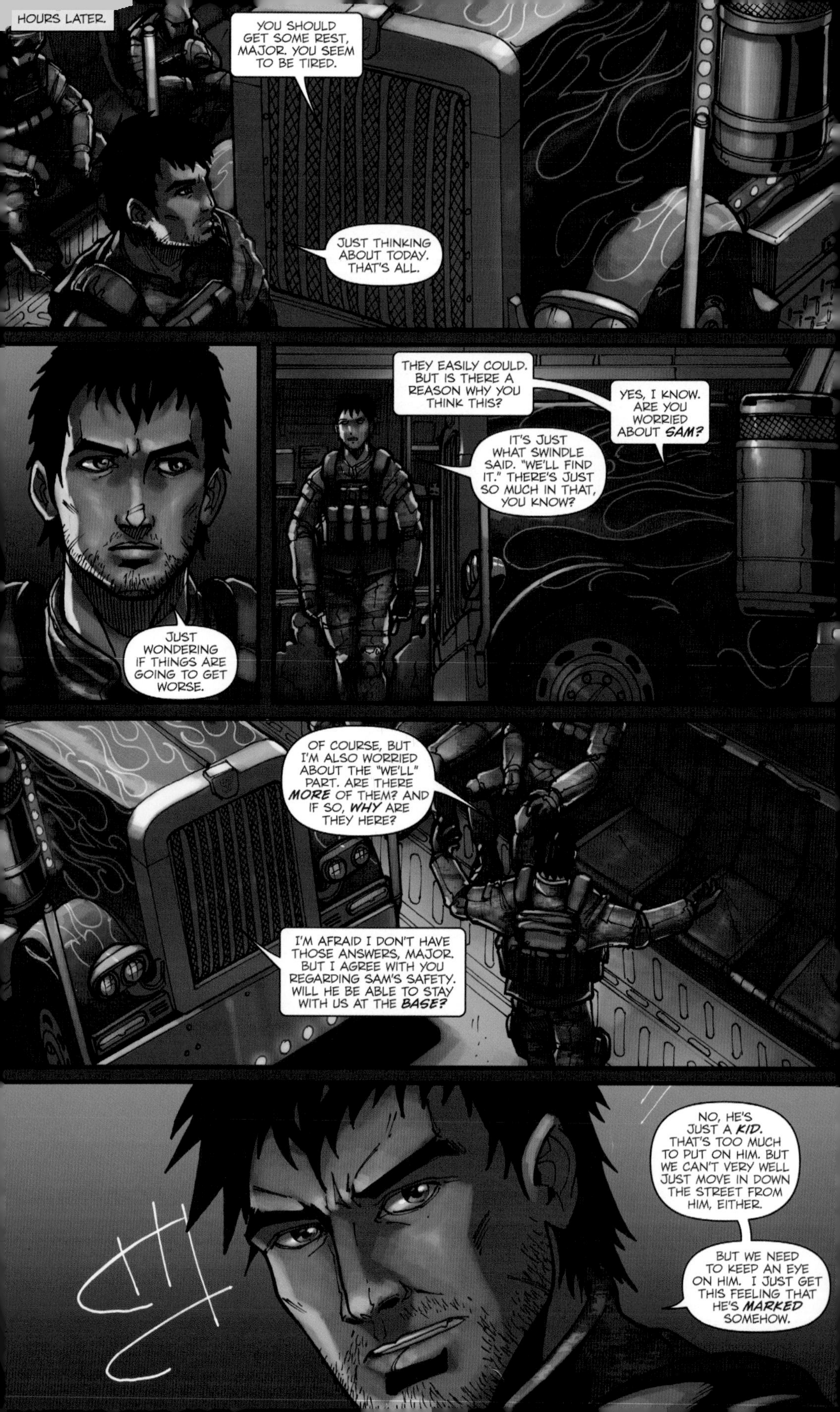
HOURS LATER.
YOU SHOULD GET SOME REST, MAJOR. YOU SEEM TO BE TIRED.
JUST THINKING ABOUT TODAY. THAT'S ALL.
JUST WONDERING IF THINGS ARE GOING TO GET WORSE.
THEY EASILY COULD. BUT IS THERE A REASON WHY YOU THINK THIS?
IT'S JUST WHAT SWINDLE SAID. "WE'LL FIND IT." THERE'S JUST SO MUCH IN THAT, YOU KNOW?
YES, I KNOW. ARE YOU WORRIED ABOUT SAM?
OF COURSE, BUT I'M ALSO WORRIED ABOUT THE "WE'LL" PART. ARE THERE MORE OF THEM? AND IF SO, WHY ARE THEY HERE?
I'M AFRAID I DON'T HAVE THOSE ANSWERS, MAJOR. BUT I AGREE WITH YOU REGARDING SAM'S SAFETY. WILL HE BE ABLE TO STAY WITH US AT THE BASE?
NO, HE'S JUST A KID. THAT'S TOO MUCH TO PUT ON HIM. BUT WE CAN'T VERY WELL JUST MOVE IN DOWN THE STREET FROM HIM, EITHER.
BUT WE NEED TO KEEP AN EYE ON HIM. I JUST GET THIS FEELING THAT HE'S MARKED SOMEHOW.

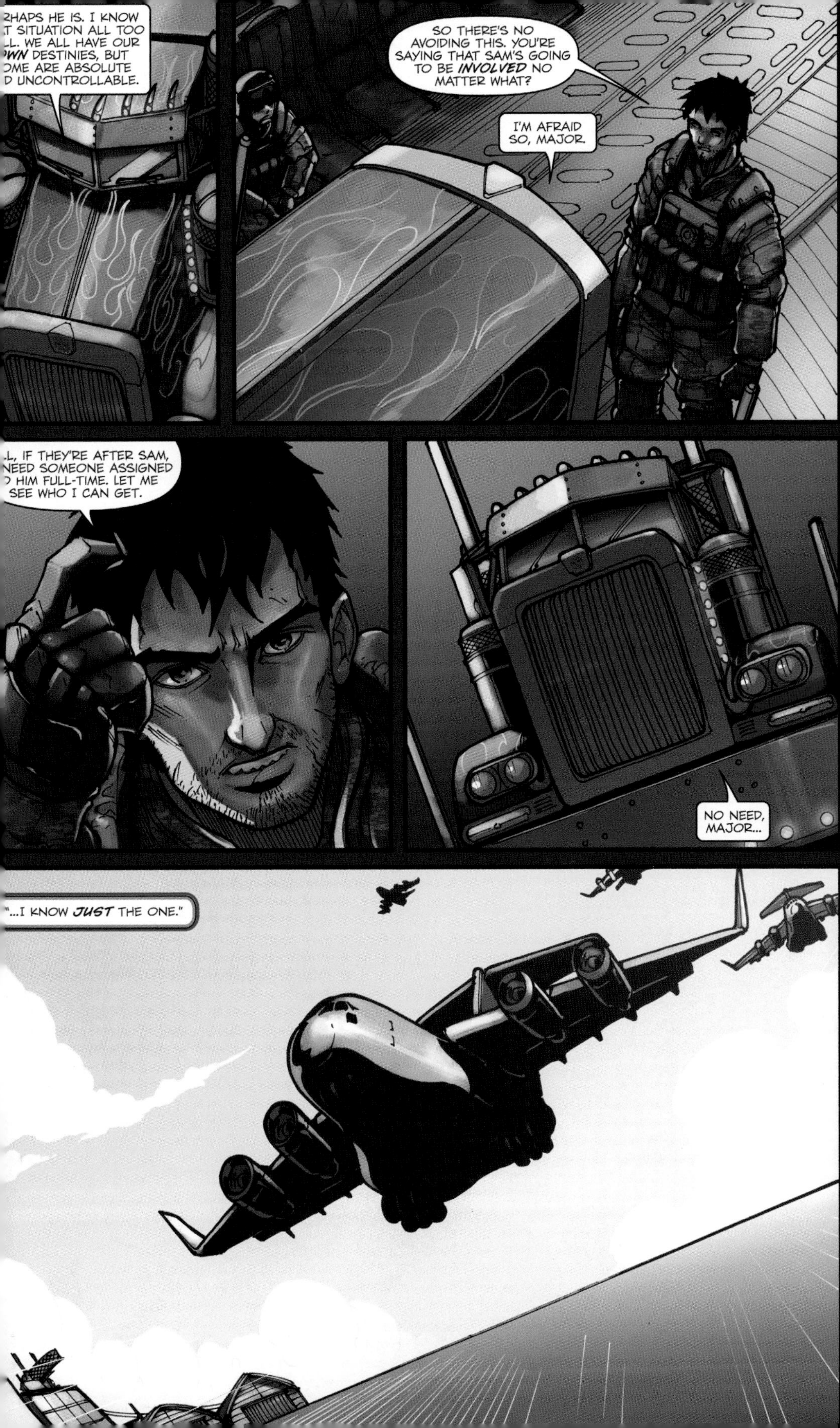

RHAPS HE IS. I KNOW
T SITUATION ALL TOO
LL. WE ALL HAVE OUR
WN DESTINIES, BUT
OME ARE ABSOLUTE
D UNCONTROLLABLE.
SO THERE'S NO AVOIDING THIS. YOU'RE SAYING THAT SAM'S GOING TO BE *INVOLVED* NO MATTER WHAT?
I'M AFRAID SO, MAJOR.
L, IF THEY'RE AFTER SAM, NEED SOMEONE ASSIGNED HIM FULL-TIME. LET ME SEE WHO I CAN GET.
NO NEED, MAJOR...
"...I KNOW *JUST* THE ONE."

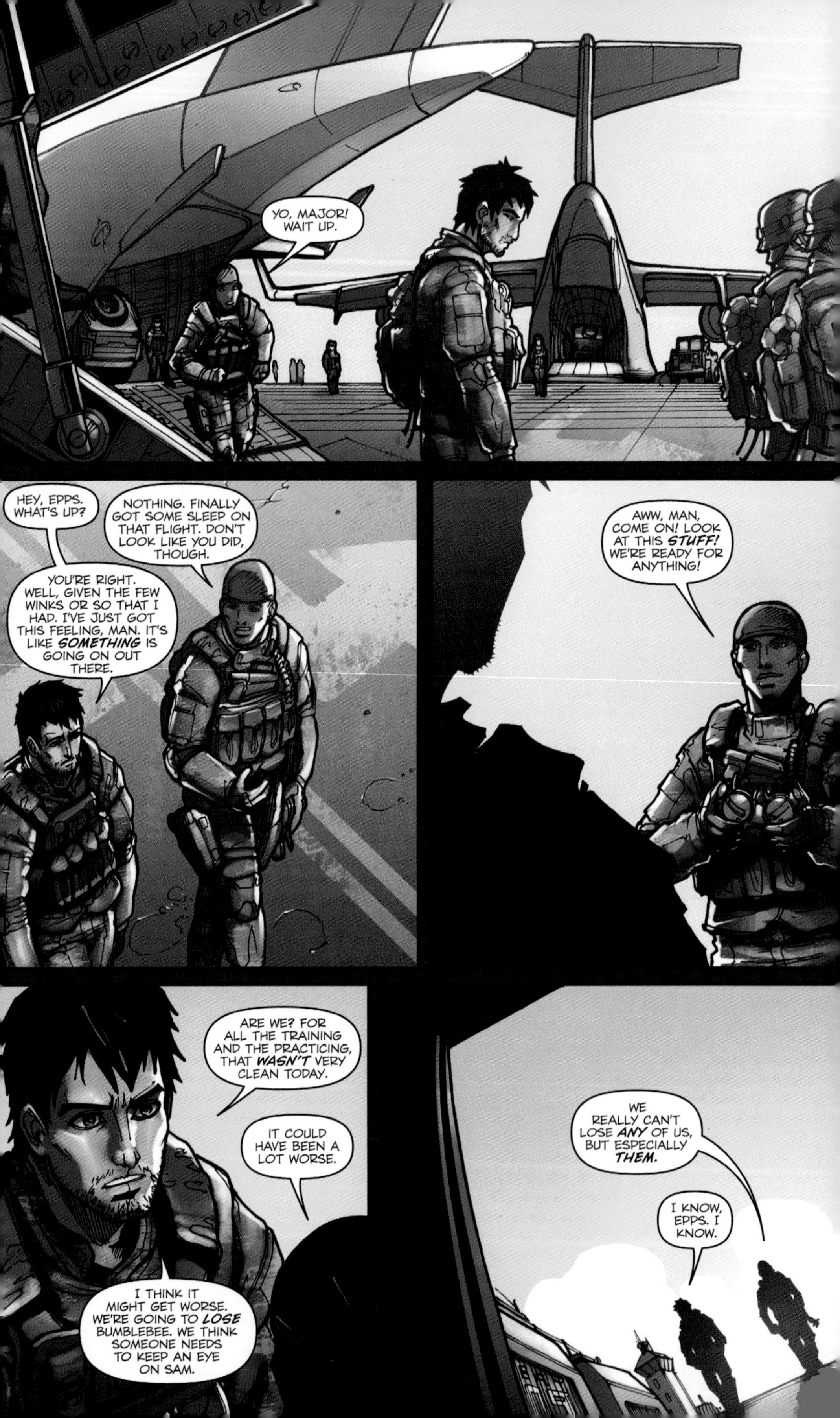
YO, MAJOR! WAIT UP.
HEY, EPPS. WHAT'S UP?
NOTHING. FINALLY GOT SOME SLEEP ON THAT FLIGHT. DON'T LOOK LIKE YOU DID, THOUGH.
YOU'RE RIGHT. WELL, GIVEN THE FEW WINKS OR SO THAT I HAD. I'VE JUST GOT THIS FEELING, MAN. IT'S LIKE SOMETHING IS GOING ON OUT THERE.
AWW, MAN, COME ON! LOOK AT THIS STUFF! WE'RE READY FOR ANYTHING!
ARE WE? FOR ALL THE TRAINING AND THE PRACTICING, THAT WASN'T VERY CLEAN TODAY.
IT COULD HAVE BEEN A LOT WORSE.
I THINK IT MIGHT GET WORSE. WE'RE GOING TO LOSE BUMBLEBEE. WE THINK SOMEONE NEEDS TO KEEP AN EYE ON SAM.
WE REALLY CAN'T LOSE ANY OF US, BUT ESPECIALLY THEM.
I KNOW, EPPS. I KNOW.

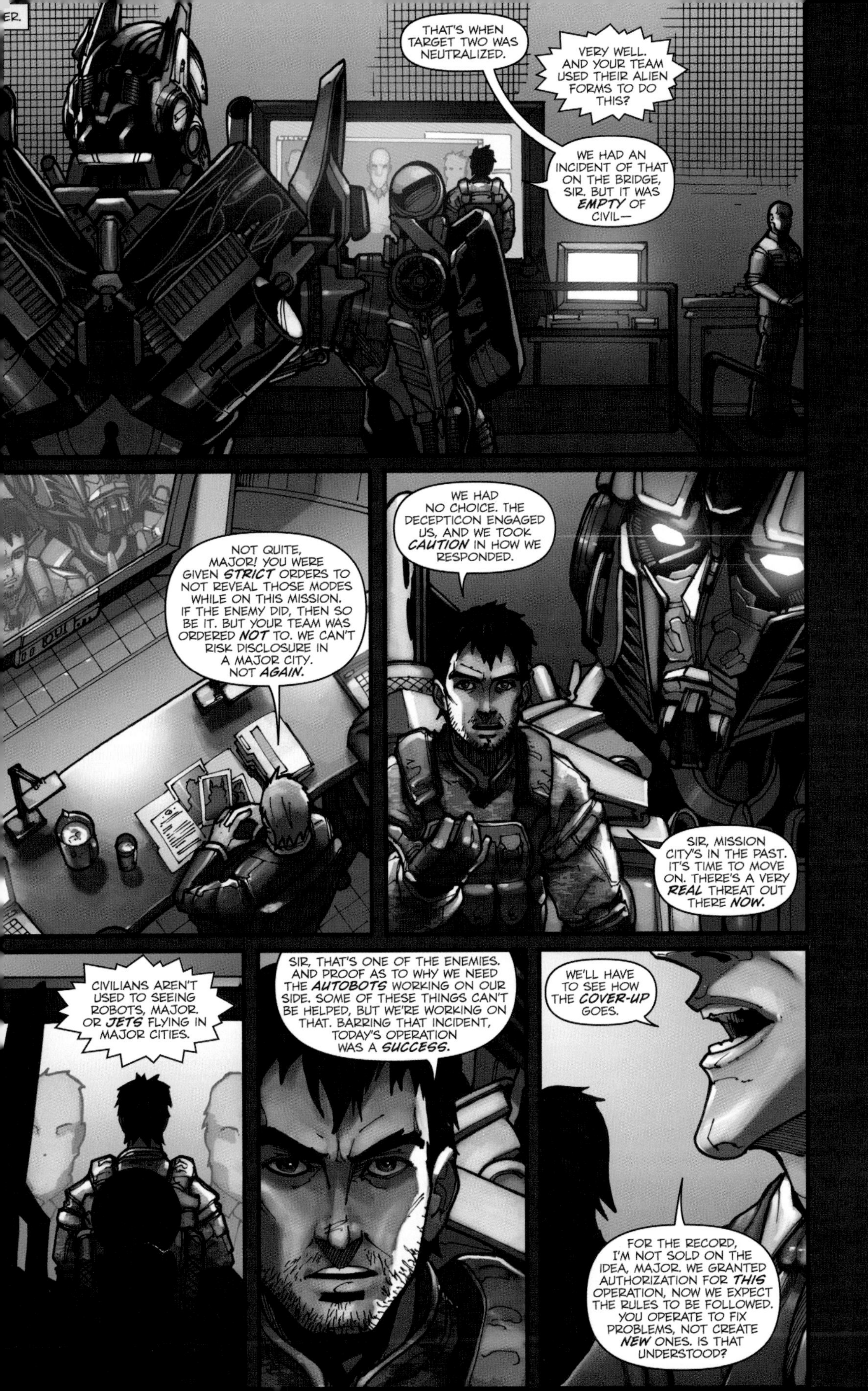
ER.
THAT'S WHEN TARGET TWO WAS NEUTRALIZED.
VERY WELL. AND YOUR TEAM USED THEIR ALIEN FORMS TO DO THIS?
WE HAD AN INCIDENT OF THAT ON THE BRIDGE, SIR. BUT IT WAS EMPTY OF CIVIL—
NOT QUITE, MAJOR! YOU WERE GIVEN STRICT ORDERS TO NOT REVEAL THOSE MODES WHILE ON THIS MISSION. IF THE ENEMY DID, THEN SO BE IT. BUT YOUR TEAM WAS ORDERED NOT TO. WE CAN'T RISK DISCLOSURE IN A MAJOR CITY. NOT AGAIN.
WE HAD NO CHOICE. THE DECEPTICON ENGAGED US, AND WE TOOK CAUTION IN HOW WE RESPONDED.
SIR, MISSION CITY'S IN THE PAST. IT'S TIME TO MOVE ON. THERE'S A VERY REAL THREAT OUT THERE NOW.
CIVILIANS AREN'T USED TO SEEING ROBOTS, MAJOR. OR JETS FLYING IN MAJOR CITIES.
SIR, THAT'S ONE OF THE ENEMIES. AND PROOF AS TO WHY WE NEED THE AUTOBOTS WORKING ON OUR SIDE. SOME OF THESE THINGS CAN'T BE HELPED, BUT WE'RE WORKING ON THAT. BARRING THAT INCIDENT, TODAY'S OPERATION WAS A SUCCESS.
WE'LL HAVE TO SEE HOW THE COVER-UP GOES.
FOR THE RECORD, I'M NOT SOLD ON THE IDEA, MAJOR. WE GRANTED AUTHORIZATION FOR THIS OPERATION, NOW WE EXPECT THE RULES TO BE FOLLOWED. YOU OPERATE TO FIX PROBLEMS, NOT CREATE NEW ONES. IS THAT UNDERSTOOD?

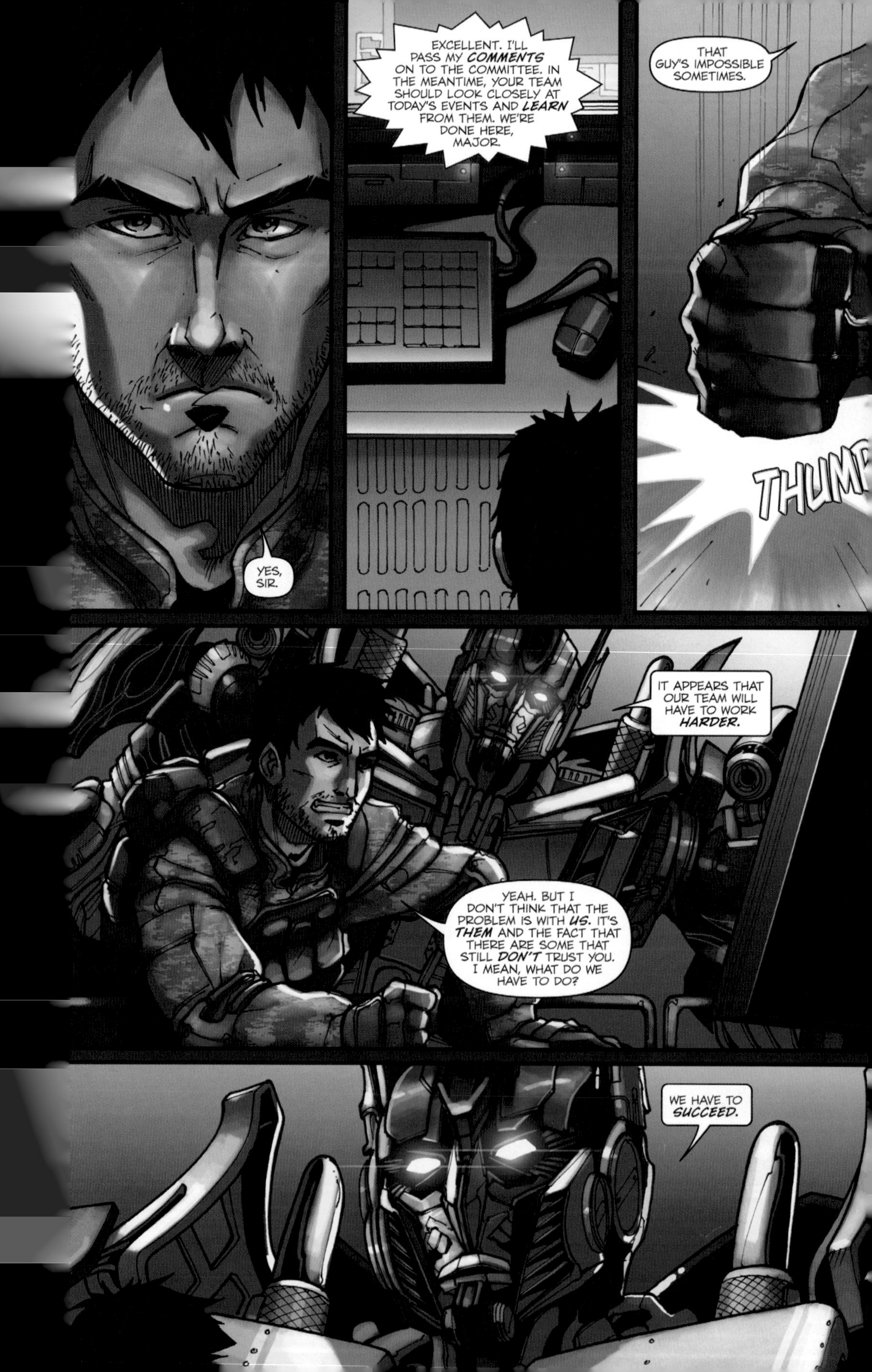
EXCELLENT. I'LL PASS MY COMMENTS ON TO THE COMMITTEE. IN THE MEANTIME, YOUR TEAM SHOULD LOOK CLOSELY AT TODAY'S EVENTS AND LEARN FROM THEM. WE'RE DONE HERE, MAJOR.
YES, SIR.
THAT GUY'S IMPOSSIBLE SOMETIMES.
THUMP
IT APPEARS THAT OUR TEAM WILL HAVE TO WORK HARDER.
YEAH. BUT I DON'T THINK THAT THE PROBLEM IS WITH US. IT'S THEM AND THE FACT THAT THERE ARE SOME THAT STILL DON'T TRUST YOU. I MEAN, WHAT DO WE HAVE TO DO?
WE HAVE TO SUCCEED.

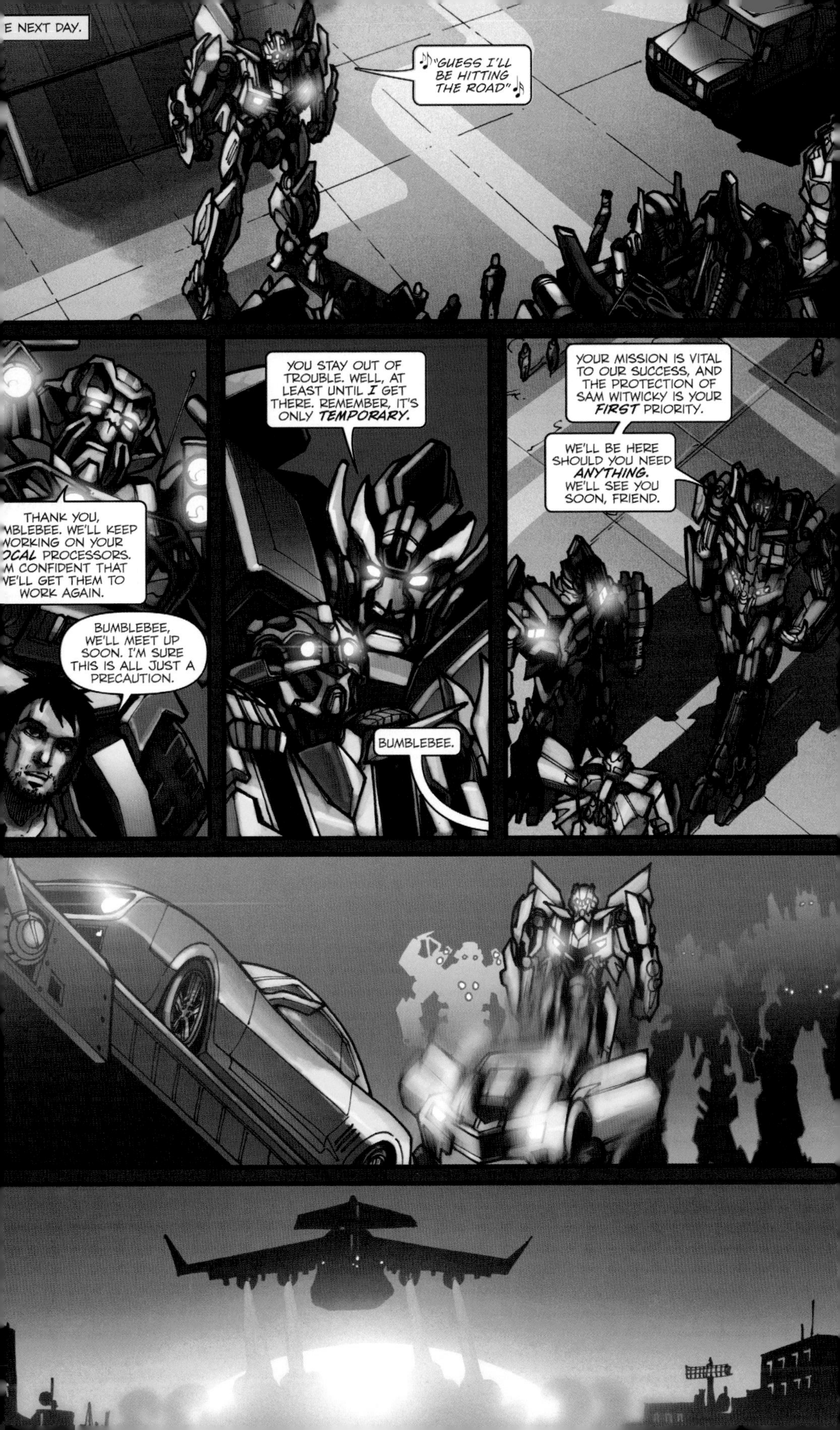
E NEXT DAY.
"GUESS I'LL BE HITTING THE ROAD"
THANK YOU, MBLEBEE. WE'LL KEEP WORKING ON YOUR OCAL PROCESSORS. M CONFIDENT THAT VE'LL GET THEM TO WORK AGAIN.
BUMBLEBEE, WE'LL MEET UP SOON. I'M SURE THIS IS ALL JUST A PRECAUTION.
YOU STAY OUT OF TROUBLE. WELL, AT LEAST UNTIL I GET THERE. REMEMBER, IT'S ONLY TEMPORARY.
BUMBLEBEE.
YOUR MISSION IS VITAL TO OUR SUCCESS, AND THE PROTECTION OF SAM WITWICKY IS YOUR FIRST PRIORITY.
WE'LL BE HERE SHOULD YOU NEED ANYTHING. WE'LL SEE YOU SOON, FRIEND.

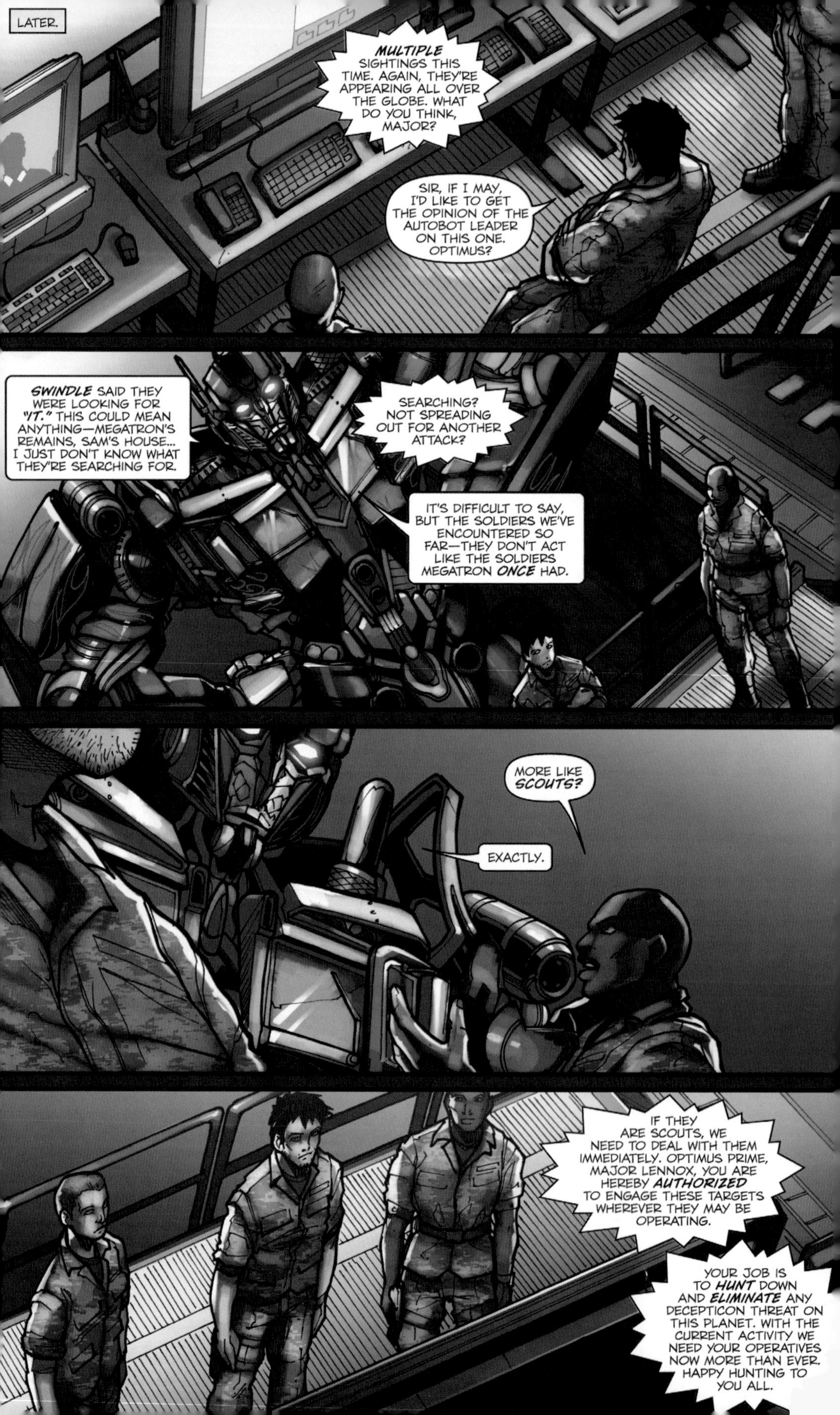
LATER.
MULTIPLE SIGHTINGS THIS TIME. AGAIN, THEY'RE APPEARING ALL OVER THE GLOBE. WHAT DO YOU THINK, MAJOR?
SIR, IF I MAY, I'D LIKE TO GET THE OPINION OF THE AUTOBOT LEADER ON THIS ONE. OPTIMUS?
SWINDLE SAID THEY WERE LOOKING FOR "IT." THIS COULD MEAN ANYTHING—MEGATRON'S REMAINS, SAM'S HOUSE... I JUST DON'T KNOW WHAT THEY'RE SEARCHING FOR.
SEARCHING? NOT SPREADING OUT FOR ANOTHER ATTACK?
IT'S DIFFICULT TO SAY, BUT THE SOLDIERS WE'VE ENCOUNTERED SO FAR—THEY DON'T ACT LIKE THE SOLDIERS MEGATRON ONCE HAD.
MORE LIKE SCOUTS?
EXACTLY.
IF THEY ARE SCOUTS, WE NEED TO DEAL WITH THEM IMMEDIATELY. OPTIMUS PRIME, MAJOR LENNOX, YOU ARE HEREBY AUTHORIZED TO ENGAGE THESE TARGETS WHEREVER THEY MAY BE OPERATING.
YOUR JOB IS TO HUNT DOWN AND ELIMINATE ANY DECEPTICON THREAT ON THIS PLANET. WITH THE CURRENT ACTIVITY WE NEED YOUR OPERATIVES NOW MORE THAN EVER. HAPPY HUNTING TO YOU ALL.

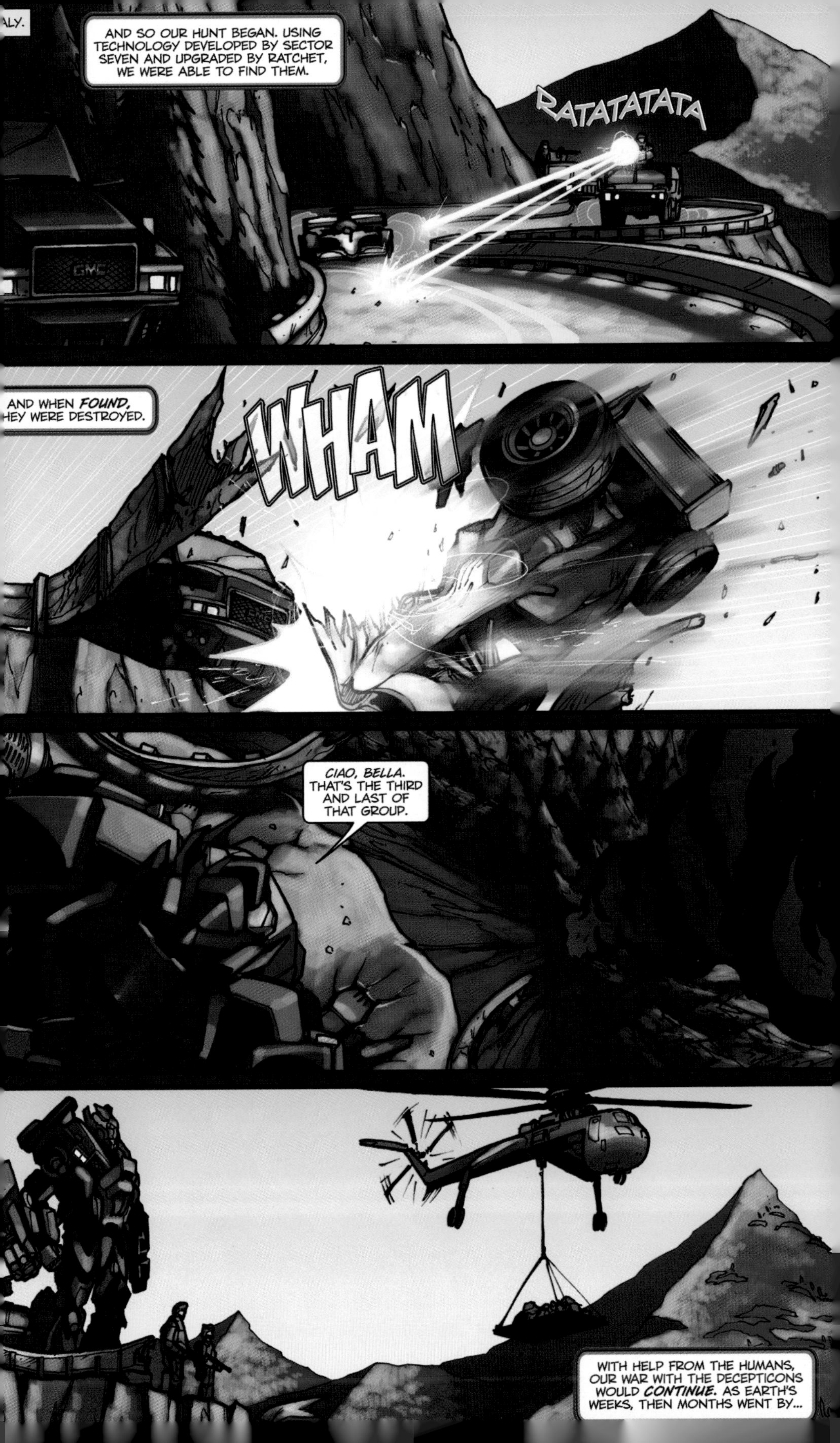
ALY.
AND SO OUR HUNT BEGAN. USING TECHNOLOGY DEVELOPED BY SECTOR SEVEN AND UPGRADED BY RATCHET, WE WERE ABLE TO FIND THEM.
RATATATATA
AND WHEN *FOUND*, HEY WERE DESTROYED.
WHAM
CIAO, BELLA. THAT'S THE THIRD AND LAST OF THAT GROUP.
WITH HELP FROM THE HUMANS, OUR WAR WITH THE DECEPTICONS WOULD ***CONTINUE.*** AS EARTH'S WEEKS, THEN MONTHS WENT BY...

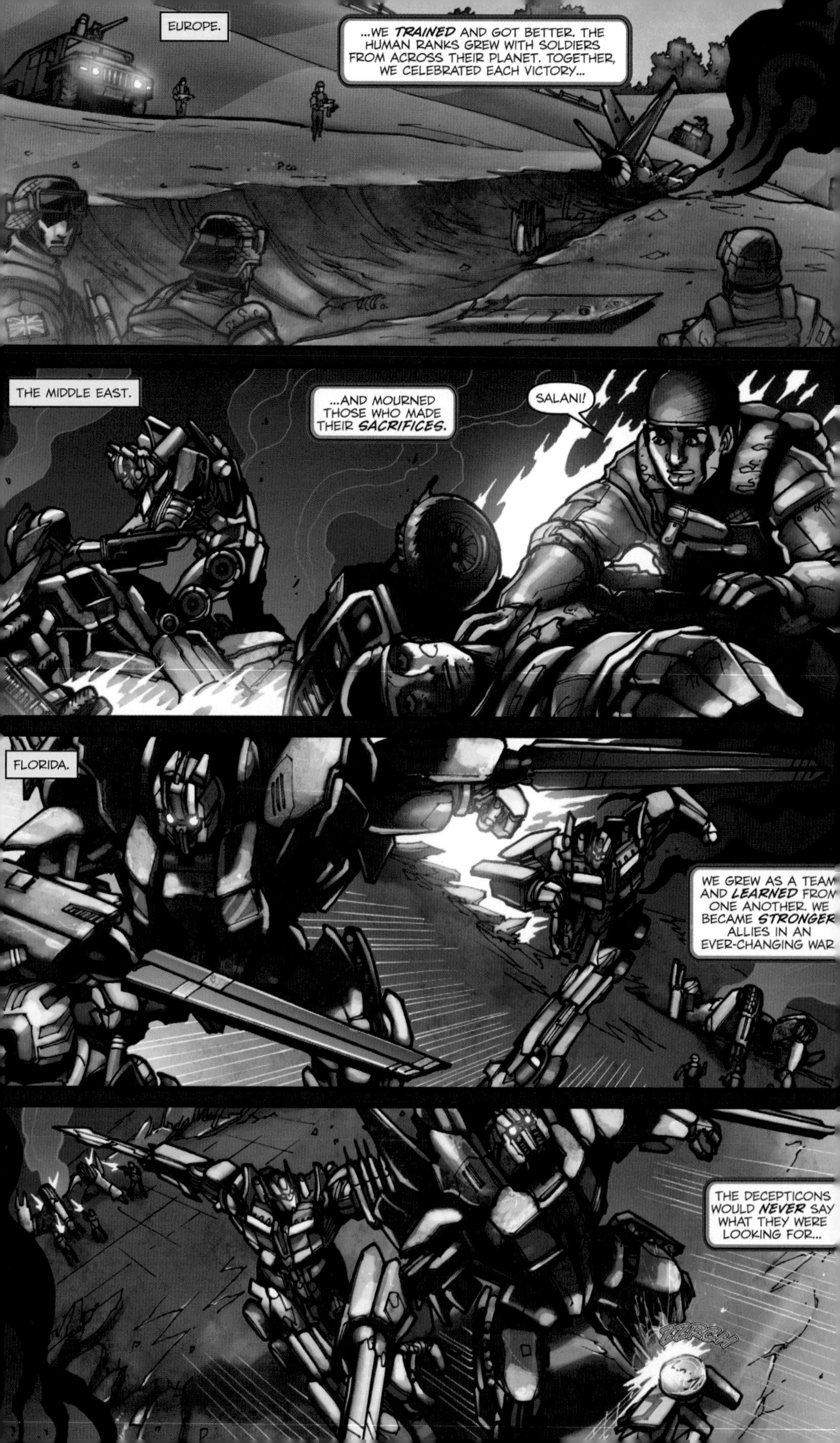
EUROPE.
...WE TRAINED AND GOT BETTER. THE HUMAN RANKS GREW WITH SOLDIERS FROM ACROSS THEIR PLANET. TOGETHER, WE CELEBRATED EACH VICTORY...
THE MIDDLE EAST.
...AND MOURNED THOSE WHO MADE THEIR SACRIFICES.
SALANI!
FLORIDA.
WE GREW AS A TEAM AND LEARNED FROM ONE ANOTHER. WE BECAME STRONGER ALLIES IN AN EVER-CHANGING WAR.
THE DECEPTICONS WOULD NEVER SAY WHAT THEY WERE LOOKING FOR...
ZZRCH

ZZZRRK

...THEY USUALLY NEVER LASTED LONG ENOUGH TO TELL US.

AND *SOME*, WE COULD NEVER SEEM TO GET RID OF.

BARRICADE GOT AWAY, PRIME. I'LL NOTIFY BUMBLEBEE.

EACH MISSION WAS FOLLOWED WITH A DEBRIEFING WITH THE HUMAN LEADERS. IT IS HERE THAT OUR TEAM RECEIVED JUDGMENT AND *NEW* ORDERS.

THE NEXT DAY.

IT WAS *THIS* BRIEFING IN PARTICULAR THAT BROUGHT US BOTH JOY AND HOPE.

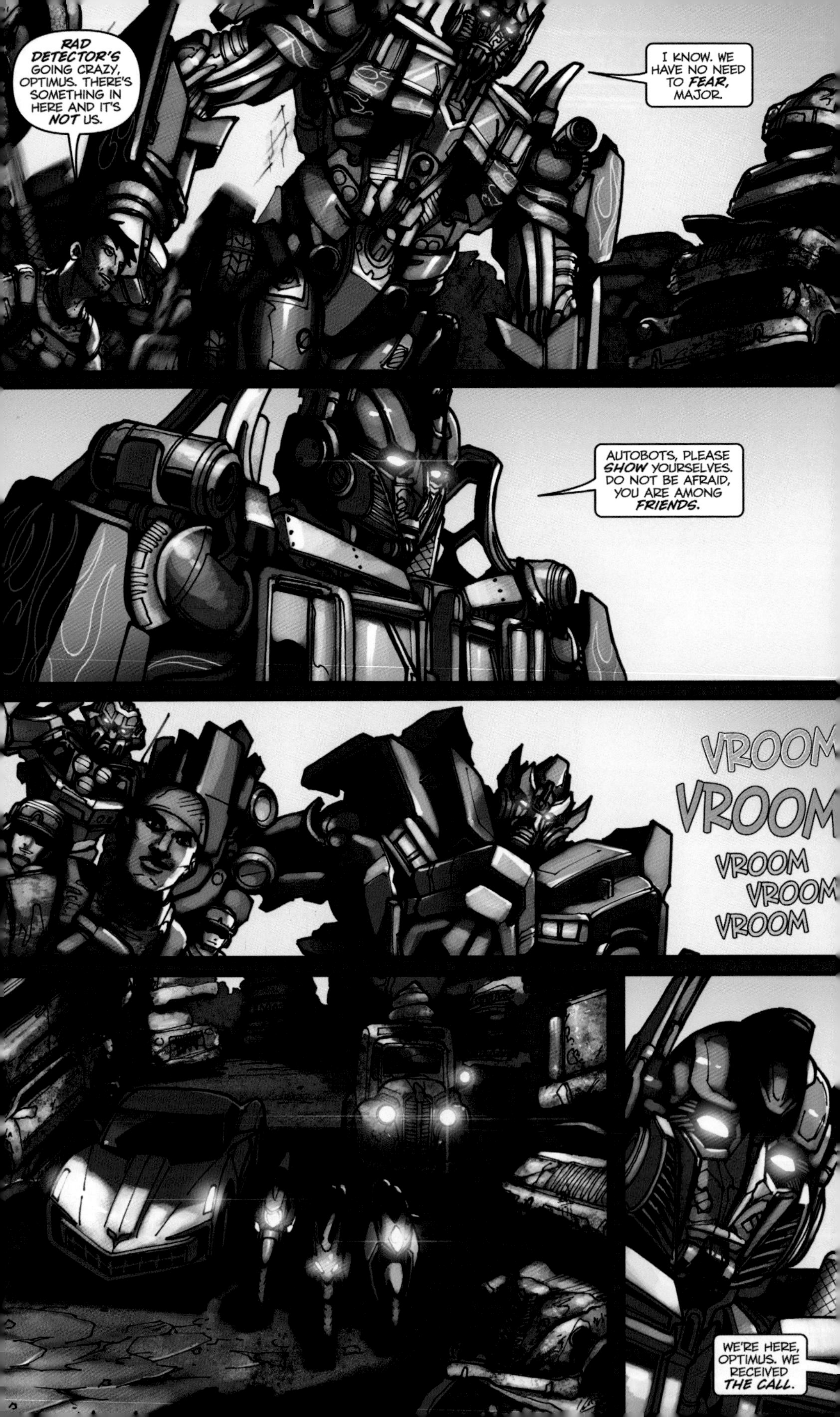

RAD DETECTOR'S GOING CRAZY, OPTIMUS. THERE'S SOMETHING IN HERE AND IT'S NOT US.
I KNOW. WE HAVE NO NEED TO FEAR, MAJOR.
AUTOBOTS, PLEASE SHOW YOURSELVES. DO NOT BE AFRAID, YOU ARE AMONG FRIENDS.
VROOM
VROOM
VROOM
VROOM
VROOM
WE'RE HERE, OPTIMUS. WE RECEIVED THE CALL.

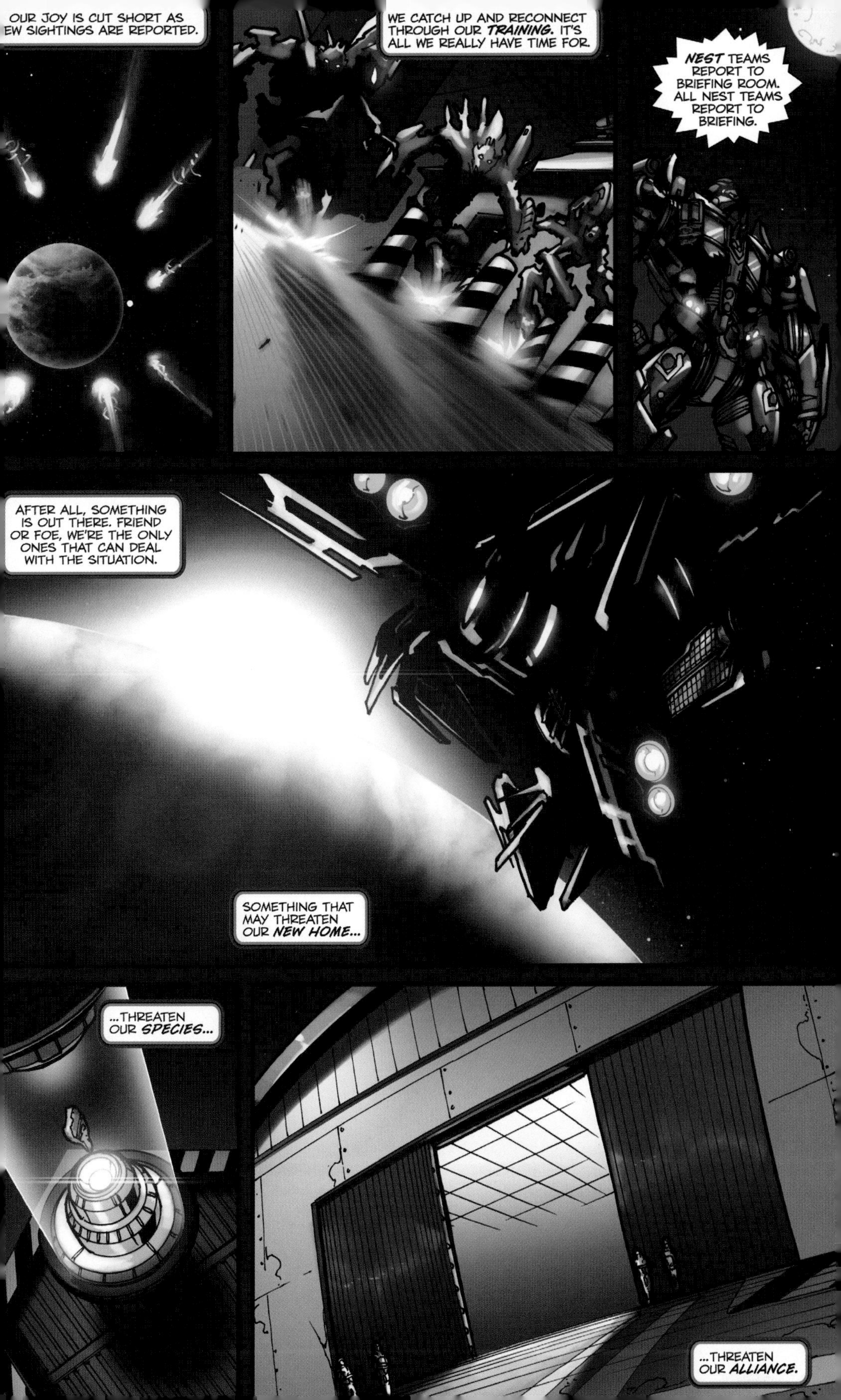
OUR JOY IS CUT SHORT AS
EW SIGHTINGS ARE REPORTED.
WE CATCH UP AND RECONNECT THROUGH OUR TRAINING. IT'S ALL WE REALLY HAVE TIME FOR.
NEST TEAMS REPORT TO BRIEFING ROOM. ALL NEST TEAMS REPORT TO BRIEFING.
AFTER ALL, SOMETHING IS OUT THERE. FRIEND OR FOE, WE'RE THE ONLY ONES THAT CAN DEAL WITH THE SITUATION.
SOMETHING THAT MAY THREATEN OUR NEW HOME...
...THREATEN OUR SPECIES...
...THREATEN OUR ALLIANCE.

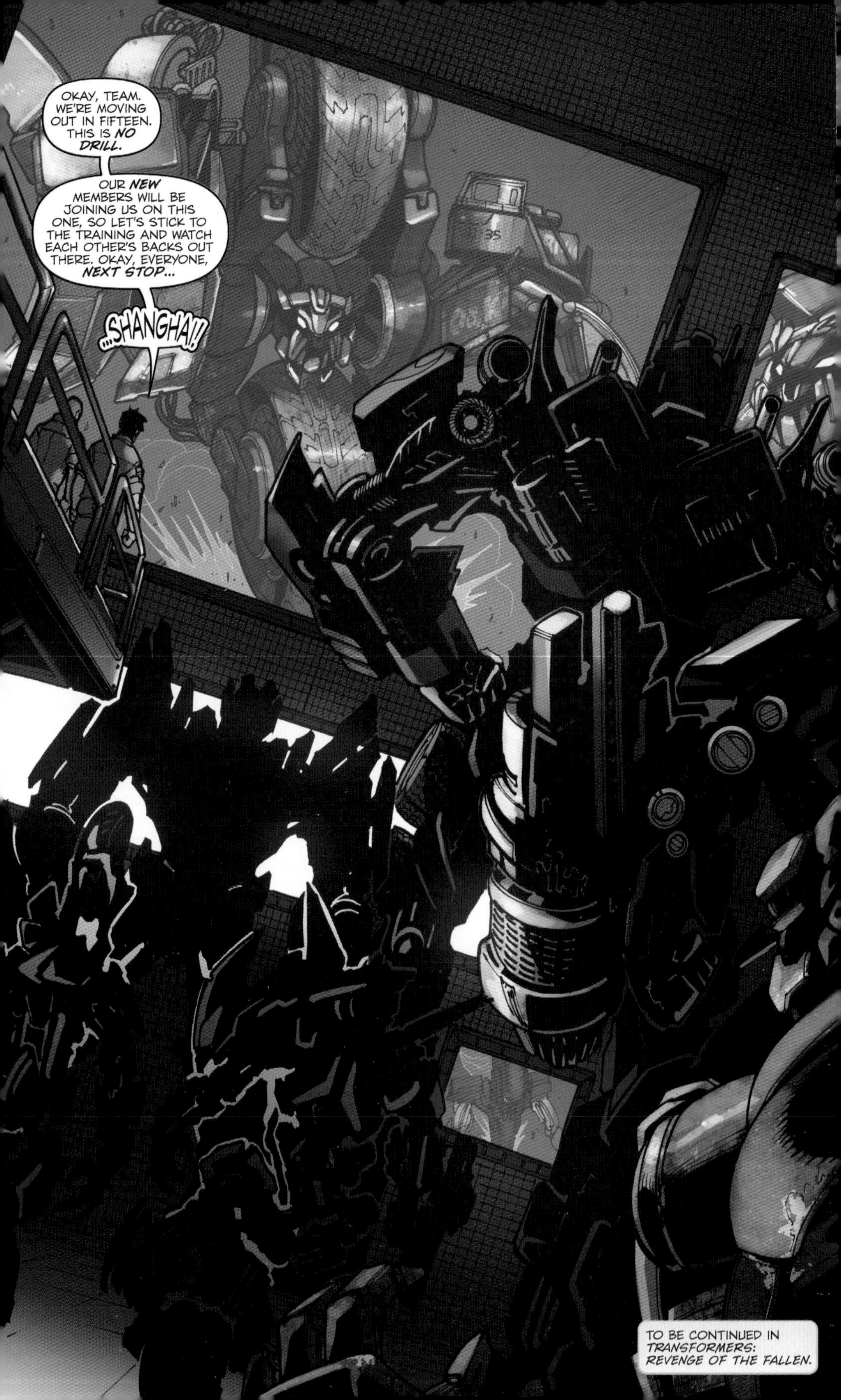
OKAY, TEAM. WE'RE MOVING OUT IN FIFTEEN. THIS IS *NO DRILL.*
OUR *NEW* MEMBERS WILL BE JOINING US ON THIS ONE, SO LET'S STICK TO THE TRAINING AND WATCH EACH OTHER'S BACKS OUT THERE. OKAY, EVERYONE, *NEXT STOP...*
...SHANGHAI!
TO BE CONTINUED IN *TRANSFORMERS: REVENGE OF THE FALLEN.*